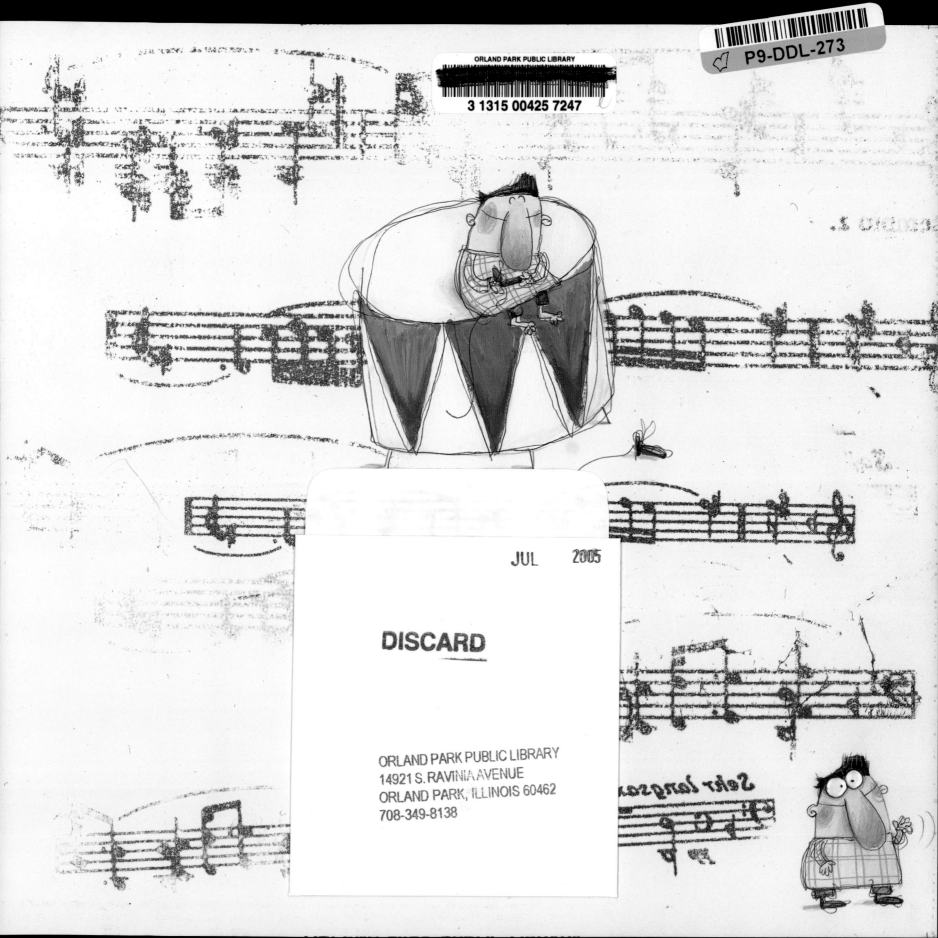

To my best friends, Caleb and Lena, for their
vivid imaginations, constant inspiration, and
frequent insillyation. And to Julie, who has
stuck by me even though I am thick and thin.
—A. M.

To everyone who has believed and still
believes in me. Special thanks to my family
to whom I have always been close.
—A. C.

Atheneum Books for Young Readers
An imprint of Simon & Schuster Children's Publishing Division
1230 Avenue of the Americas, New York, New York 10020
Text copyright © 2005 by Alan Madison
Illustrations copyright © 2005 by AnnaLaura Cantone

Book design by Lee Wade
The text for this book is set in Graham.
Manufactured in China
First Edition
10 9 8 7 6 5 4 3 2 1
Library of Congress Cataloging-in-Publication Data
Madison, Alan.
Pecorino's first concert / Alan Madison ; illustrated by AnnaLaura
Cantone.— 1st ed.
p. cm.
"An Anne Schwartz Book."
Summary: Everyone thinks that Pecorino Sasquatch is the silliest
boy in the world, and he proves them right when he and his mother
go to hear a concert conducted by the great Pimplelini.
ISBN 0-689-85952-X
[1. Concerts—Fiction. 2. Humorous stories.]
I. Cantone, AnnaLaura, ill. II. Title.
PZ7.M5287 Pe 2005
[E]—dc21
2002014167

Alan Madison and AnnaLaura Cantone present

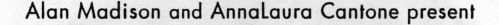

pecorino's

FiRST conCERT

An Anne Schwartz Book   Atheneum Books for Young Readers   New York London Toronto Sydney

Everyone thought Pecorino Sasquatch was the silliest boy in the world. He was so silly that when it was cold he wore shorts and when it was hot he wore mittens. He was so silly that he would fall asleep in the day and wake up at night.

One day Pecorino's mother, Mrs. Sasquatch, proclaimed, "Dearest dumpling, today we are going to a concert."

Pecorino was so excited he rabbit-hopped around his room. Then he froze statue still. "What's a concert?" he asked.

"A concert," explained his mother, "is when a group of musicians make music. And this concert is special because the world-famous conductor Vittorio Pimplelini, who has traveled all the way from Pimplelonia, will be conducting."

Pecorino and Mrs. Sasquatch got on the bus that went through the great, green park to the concert hall. The bus was crowded and there was only one seat left, next to a large man with a long mustache. Pecorino stared up at the bushy black hairs that burst from under the man's nose and came to rest on his shirt. He imagined the man raking his mustache each morning to keep it clean, watering it every afternoon to make it grow, and pruning it at night to keep it trim.

"Young man, it is quite rude to stare," said the mustached man. "What is it that you want?"

"I want a new bicycle," Pecorino answered.

"That is not what I meant," fumphered the fellow. "I want to know what you're goggling at."

"Sir, I am not gargling anything," replied Pecorino politely.

The man was so perplexed and furmuzzled that he stormed off the bus and into the great, green park, his wondrous mustache warbling in the wind.

The bus dropped Pecorino and his mother right under the brightly colored banners of the great concert hall.

Inside, except for one old man who skittered up and down the aisles like a chased cockroach, it was empty. "You're early. Very early. Sit down. Down," repeated the cockroach man in his insect voice before skedaddling away.

And so Pecorino sat. The colossal room was carrot-colored from floor to ceiling. "Pecorino," his mother said, "I have to go to the ladies' room. I expect to find you in this chair when I return."

Except for the many musical instruments sleeping onstage, Pecorino was alone. But from his orange velvet seat, he could barely see the bright, brown violins and the sleek, silver flutes.

He stood up, just to get a better look.

"Come closer!" he heard the trumpets trill. He tippytoed toward the stage.

"You must see us!" he heard the cymbals sing. He climbed the three steps.

"Play us!" the piccolos piped in.

Pecorino stepped onto the stage.

Now Pecorino no longer felt alone. He patted the bass drum. *Bip, bap, bop.*

He plucked a few notes on the cello. *Tink, tank, tunk.*

He floated a few notes on the flute. *Whistle, wassle, woooooo . . .*

And then he put his lips to the tuba . . . and blew.

Not a single sound came out.

He tried again—with an extra deep breath.

Still nothing.

Maybe something is stuck inside, thought Pecorino. He climbed onto a chair and looked into the tuba's deep wide bell.

"Hello," called Pecorino.

"Hello," a voice called back.

Maybe a little boy is inside the tuba, thought Pecorino.

"Are you stuck?" he called down.

"Stuck?" he heard.

Pecorino leaned farther over the instrument.

"Give me your hand."

"Give me your hand"
came bouncing back.

"Here it is!"
cried Pecorino, reaching down inside.

"Here it is!"
repeated the tuba.

Pecorino stretched and squirmed and wiggled closer until . . . he fell headfirst into the tuba!
"Help!" Pecorino yelled. But not a single sound came out.

When Mrs. Sasquatch returned,
Pecorino was gone.

"Dearest dumpling," she sang.
"Darling boy?" she shouted.

"PECORINO!"

she shrieked. But there was no answer.

Inside and upside down, Pecorino tried to push himself out with his hands. He tried to pull himself out with his feet. He tried to wiggle, wossle, and wamboodle himself out using every part of his body from his tongue to his toenails. But he didn't move an inch. Pecorino worried that he'd have to live in the tuba his whole life, or at least until he grew tall enough for someone to see his feet sticking out of the top.

The concert hall filled with people.

There was a thunder of applause for the world-famous Vittorio Pimplelini, who had traveled all the way from Pimplelonia. Pimplelini tapped his slender baton on the podium. *Click, click, click.*

Silence.

"Wait!" The man from the bus with the droopy black mustache tumbled onto the stage.

Pimplelini scowled.

"Sorry, Maestro. I had to walk across the whole great, green park to get here," the late tuba player huffed as he hoisted the heavy instrument onto his lap.

Pimplelini turned to the drums and swung his baton up in the air. The drummer drummed. He spun to the violins, swung his baton down to the floor, and the violinists violined. The music vibrated around Pecorino, who was sure he would have liked the concert better if he weren't upside down.

The baton pointed, and soon the clarinets, coronets, castanets, flutes, French horns, fiddles, piccolos, pipes, trumpets, trombones, triangle, and zither had all joined in. World-famous Pimplelonian conductor Vittorio Pimplelini jumped and swirled, hopped and whirled, his carefully combed hair whipping back and forth as the music became louder and faster, faster and louder.

At last it was time for the tuba to play. Pimplelini pointed his baton. The musician took a deep breath, pressed his lips to the mouthpiece, blew, and . . .

Not a single sound came out.

Pimplelini aimed his baton at the tuba again.

Still nothing.

The tuba player's mustache began to warble across his face. *The audience is being quite rude staring at me*, he thought. *What is it that they want?* But he knew. And so with a deep, deep breath he let loose a Brobdingnagian blow. His face turned more carroty than the carpet, a humongous HARUMPH rang out . . .

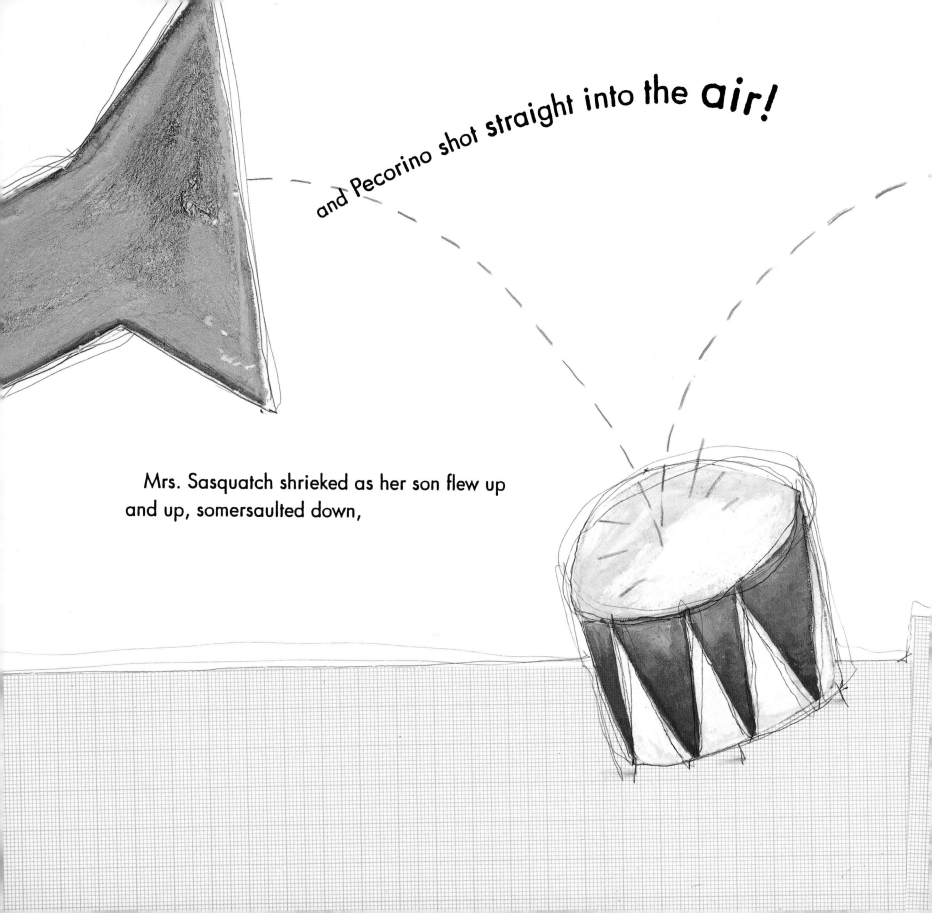

and Pecorino shot straight into the **air!**

Mrs. Sasquatch shrieked as her son flew up and up, somersaulted down,

bounced off the big bass drum
with a *BOOM-de-boom*, sailed over
the audience . . .

and landed right in his mother's arms.

The audience clapped and clapped! The tuba player lay on the floor gasping for breath. And Conductor Vittorio Pimplelini, furious, stomped off the stage and did not stop until he reached Pimplelonia.

Mrs. Sasquatch hugged her son.

"There's another boy in that tuba," declared Pecorino.
"We have to save him."

"Dearest dumpling, one day your imagination is
going to get you into trouble," whispered his
mother.

"He would never do that,"
Pecorino replied. "We're best
friends."

Then Mrs. Sasquatch took her
son's hand and together they headed off
for home.